Usher Parsons

# Sketches of Rhode Island Physicians Deceased prior to 1850

Anatiposi

**Usher Parsons**

# Sketches of Rhode Island Physicians Deceased prior to 1850

Reprint of the original.

1st Edition 2023 | ISBN: 978-3-38230-158-3

Anatiposi Verlag is an imprint of Outlook Verlagsgesellschaft mbH.

Verlag (Publisher): Outlook Verlag GmbH, Zeilweg 44, 60439 Frankfurt, Deutschland
Vertretungsberechtigt (Authorized to represent): E. Roepke, Zeilweg 44, 60439 Frankfurt, Deutschland
Druck (Print): Books on Demand GmbH, In de Tarpen 42, 22848 Norderstedt, Deutschland

# SKETCHES

OF

# RHODE ISLAND PHYSICIANS,

## DECEASED PRIOR TO 1850:

PREPARED BY

USHER PARSONS,

For the Rhode Island Medical Society.

PROVIDENCE:
KNOWLES, ANTHONY & CO., PRINTERS.
1859.

# TRANSACTIONS

OF THE

# RHODE-ISLAND MEDICAL SOCIETY.

---

VOL. I.

---

PROVIDENCE:
KNOWLES, ANTHONY & CO., PRINTERS.
1859.

# HISTORY OF THE MEDICAL PROFESSION

IN

# RHODE ISLAND.

---

At a stated meeting of the Rhode Island Medical Society, 1859, it was voted that a committee be raised to select and publish such papers now in the archives of the Society, as they may deem worthy of preservation; and also to prepare a sketch of the lives of eminent deceased physicians, from the first settlement of the colony, with an account of the medical institutions, and of other matters pertaining to the history of medicine in Rhode Island.

The committee, consisting of Usher Parsons, Isaac Ray and George L. Collins, after due consideration, have arrived at the conclusion, that the sketches and historical matters should, in the order of arrangement for publication, precede, and serve as an introduction to the first volume of papers, selected from the archives of the Society.

## SKETCHES OF THE LIVES OF EARLY PHYSICIANS.

The sketches are confined to physicians who deceased or retired from practice prior to 1850,— the only exception being that of Dr. Levi Wheaton, who died in 1852, but whose long professional career virtually terminated two years previously to his death. It is proper to observe that three or four distinguished physicians of Providence, who died between 1830 and 50, have been noticed with brevity; which is not from any want of respect for their memories, but because they were personally known to a majority of the Society, who are as capable of appreciating their high character and worth as your committee; and, because such biographical notices should come from the pen not of cotemporaries and competitors in the profession, who must incur the imputation of partiality or prejudice, but from subsequent writers, whose minds are unbiased by either, and who, by delay, would be able to add to the already accumulated facts and incidents proper to introduce. We shall commence with the founder of Newport.

JOHN CLARKE, the first physician, arrived in Boston in 1631, and resided there till 1638. He then removed to Portsmouth, the north part of Rhode Island, and in the following year to Newport. In 1651 he went to England, where he united with Roger Williams in procuring the revocation of Coddington's commission as governor of the islands in Narragansett bay. Williams returned with the revocation, but Clarke remained twelve years in London in the practice of his profession. In this time he procured the late Charter of Rhode Island, which continued in force until 1842, when it was superseded by the present State Constitution. He afterwards returned to Newport, where he officiated as pastor of the first Baptist church, meanwhile practicing physic, until his death, which occurred April 20th, 1676, in the 68th year of his age. A full and very interesting memoir of him, by Dr. David King, is contained in the archives of the Rhode Island Historical Society.

ROBERT JEFFRIES was authorized "to exercise the functions of surgery," by the government of the Island, in 1641, and soon after Dr. JOHN CRANSTON was also licensed, with the privilege of dealing in drugs and medicines; and after him, in

1687, came Dr. SAMUEL AYRAULT, a Huguenot from New Rochelle, and practiced a few years.

Dr. THOMAS RODMAN arrived in Newport 1680, and performed professional duty until his death, in 1727, being then 80 years old. He had two wives; the first died 1690, aged 35, and his second 1732, aged 66 years. The town encouraged him in practice by a grant of land. His son, Dr. CLARKE RODMAN, was many years in active professional life, and WILLIAM RODMAN, son of Clarke and grandson of Thomas, died the year after his father, in early life. There were also three Vignerons, in succession, viz.: —

NORBENT FELICIEN VIGNERON, a native of Provence d' Artois, in France, arrived in 1690, and died 1764, at the age of nearly 95 years. He was well educated, and a popular practitioner. Many of his lineal descendants survive, but the name, it is believed, has become extinct. The late Commodore William Vigneron Taylor and his grandchild of the same name, are descended from him. CHARLES ANTONIO VIGNERON, son of Norbent, was born in Newport, and resided in Spring street. He studied with his father, and attained to eminence. He married a Miss Irish, and had five sons and three daughters. He died in New York, of small pox by inoculation, in 1772, at the age of fifty. He had a son named STEPHEN VIGNERON, Surgeon of a privateer, who was lost at sea.

Doctors JAMES NOYES, BENJAMIN STAUNTON and JONATHAN ROBINSON, the first died 1718, aged 40; the second in 1760, at an advanced age, and the third still later.

JOHN BRETT, from Germany, a pupil of Boerhaave, and a particular friend and associate of Redwood, who coöperated with him in establishing the Redwood Library, to which he left a portion of his books, and some are now to be found in private medical libraries in Newport.

From 1720 to 1760, the town of Newport was the most populous of any except Boston, in New England, and its inhabitants were better educated. Its salubrious climate attracted persons of distinction from foreign shores, among whom was Dean Berkeley, bishop of Cloyne, and many opulent Jewish merchants, and also several eminent physicians. In 1750 came Doctors William Hunter, Thomas Moffatt, from Scotland, and soon after Doctors John Halliburton and David Oliphant, all highly educated, and subsequently eminent practitioners.

Dr. William Hunter, above mentioned, arrived in 1752, from Edinburg, where he had been a pupil of the elder Monro. He practiced in Newport twenty-four years, and was the first male accoucheur in the colony. Dr. Hunter gave lectures on anatomy in 1754, 5 and 6, which were the first given on medical science in America. Advertisements of them may be seen in the Boston papers of that day. He was appointed surgeon of the troops sent to Canada, in the French war. As an operative surgeon, his skill was superior to that of his cotemporaries, he having served in the British army. He owned the largest medical library in the province, a portion of which was given by his son, the late Hon. William Hunter, to Brown University.

Dr. Thomas Moffatt was highly educated, but less successful in gaining patronage than some others. This induced him to set up a Scotch snuff manufactory, in Narragansett, in company with the father of Gilbert Stuart, the distinguished portrait painter, where the latter passed his early years. Dr. Moffatt came from Scotland about 1750, and practiced some until 1772, when his strong tory principles drove him from the country. His house was mobbed and much of his property destroyed, on account of his agency in favor of the stamp act.

Dr. John Halliburton arrived in Newport about 1750, as surgeon of a British frigate, commanded by Lord Colville. He became attached to Miss Brenton, a lady of high family connexions, and resigning his commission, he married her. By an extensive practice added to his wife's fortune, he became wealthy. He was inclined to espouse the British cause in the early part of the revolution, and was closely watched. After the enemy left Newport for Long Island and New York, a person appeared to him, who had been the bearer of letters between him and the enemy containing secret intelligence, and demanded hush money. Finding himself in his power, the doctor paid what he demanded; but the fellow soon made his appearance again, demanding a larger sum. He was told to call the following day; but in the night the doctor cleared out for Long Island in a sail-boat, and thence proceeded to New York, where the British commander offered him his choice of a hospital surgeoncy there or in Halifax, the latter of which he accepted, and his family joined him the next year, including a child named Brenton. He was appointed to the council board of the province, and died in 1807. His son Brenton was educated to the law in England, and was, for a few years, captain of a company; but he resigned and returned to the practice of law in Nova Scotia. He was appointed a judge; then one of His Majesty's council, and Chief Justice of the province, and recently received the honor of Knighthood, at the age of eighty-three. He was not the author of Sam Slick and other books, as is generally supposed, his only writings for the press being fugitive pieces in journals, and recently, when eighty years old, a pleasing poem.

Dr. David Oliphant was many years in extensive practice, and died in 1802, aged 82 years. His wife, Ann Vernon, died in July, 1826, aged 75 years. His descendants in New York are eminent merchants.

Dr. Robert Hooper, of whom little is known, died at an advanced age in 1765.

Dr. Isaac Senter, an eminent physician in Newport, was a native of London lerry, New Hampshire, born 1753. After receiving a preliminary education, he sought medical instruction, in Newport, under Dr. Moffatt. While pursuing his studies, the news of the battle of Lexington arrived, in April,

1775, which roused him in common sympathy with the citizens of the State. He joined the Rhode Island troops as surgeon, and marched to Cambridge, and was commissioned as such in the organization of the army. He accompanied General Arnold to Quebec, through Kennebec river, and the dense wilderness, which occupied thirty-two days in the inclement months of November and December, before they reached the settlements on the Chaudiere, during which they suffered incredible hardships and privations. In the assault on Quebec, all Arnold's division were either killed or captured, among whom was young Senter, who, after being detained some time to attend the sick and wounded, was released and permitted to return home. In 1779 he quitted the army, and settled as a physician at Pawtuxet in Rhode Island. He was soon after elected one of the representatives to the General Assembly. In 1780 he was appointed Surgeon and Physician General of the State, and in the same year removed to Newport, where he resumed the duties of his profession under very favorable auspices, nearly all the old physicians of eminence having died or removed during the war. He had many pupils, one only of whom, Dr. William G. Shaw, of Wickford, still survives. He contributed some able papers to European journals, was elected Fellow of the London, and of the Massachusetts Medical Societies, and of the Historical Society. In the height of his fame and usefulness he was seized with a disease which proved fatal, on the 10th of December, 1799, at the age of 46 years. Dr Senter was tall, erect and noble-looking in person, and his dignified step and bearing often arrested the attention of strangers he passed in the street. He was undoubtedly a man of high endowments, and well educated for his day.

Dr. Sylvester Gardner was born in South Kingstown, 1717, and educated under the superintendence of his brother-in-law, Rev. Dr. McSparren, and pursued his studies in medicine in France and England. He settled in Boston, and by his profession and speculation in eastern lands, he amassed great wealth. He left the country as a loyalist, and had his property confiscated. On the restoration of peace, he returned to Newport and practiced medicine three or four years, until his death, which occurred in 1786, in his 80th year. He was grandfather of the late Rev. Dr. Gardner, of Boston.

Dr. JONATHAN EASTON commenced his professional career ten years before the revolution, and continued it nearly fifty years. He was an original Fellow of the Rhode Island Medical Society. He inoculated three persons for small pox, in 1772, being the first cases in Rhode Island. His figure was tall and spare, and he dressed in the garb of a Quaker.

Dr. JONATHAN EASTON, Jr., son of the last, moved from Newport to Cumberland. He was an original Fellow of the Medical Society.

Dr. WILLIAM FLETCHER was engaged in the profession about three years in Newport, where he arrived from Lancaster, England, 1785.

There were also the following practitioners, before and after the revolution, of whom little can be gathered:— Drs. AYERS, BARTLETT and WILLIAMS, of Newport, and Drs. JARRETT and FARNSWORTH, of Middletown.

Dr. BENJAMIN MASON enjoyed the benefit of European instruction, and flourished many years before the close of the last century. He was an honorary Fellow of the Massachusetts Medical Society, and was at the head of the profession in Newport.

To the foregoing, it may be proper to add the two distinguished men who practiced in Newport for a time and removed to Boston, viz.:— Drs. SAMUEL DANFORTH and BENJAMIN WATERHOUSE. They arrived to the ages of ninety and ninety-two years. The former pursued what may be termed the "heroic practice," prescribing large doses and other energetic treatment. He attained to great eminence, and was regarded as the Hercules of the profession. His hight was over six feet, his features very prominent, and his lofty bearing commanding and dignified.

Dr. Waterhouse was a native of Newport, where he resided and studied with Dr. Halliburton. In 1775, he was sent to London, as a pupil to the celebrated Dr. Fothergill, a maternal relation. After pursuing his studies there and in Edinburg, he went to Leyden, where he graduated as Doctor of Medicine. On his return to his native land, he was elected to a professorship in Harvard, and subsequently to that of Botany in Brown University. He was ardently attached to the profession of medicine, as well as its kindred sciences, particularly Botany, in which he acquired a high reputation. In 1811, he published a work entitled the "Botanist," dedicated to the elder President Adams, written in an attractive style, and displaying high attainments. He wrote extensively for the press, and, in 1831, a work on the question of the authorship of "Junius;" but it failed to attract much interest. The doctor introduced vaccination into America, employing it first on his own children. He held the office of Surgeon of the Marine Hospital at Charlestown, and, during the war of 1812, was Hospital Surgeon in the army. He wrote extensively on politics, and was a great admirer of Jefferson and Adams.

At the beginning of the present century several cotemporaries of the medical profession occupied the field in Newport, viz.:— William Turner, David King, Edmund T. Waring, Benjamin W. Case and Enoch Hazzard, all of whom were original members in 1812. Some of these will be particularly noticed hereafter.

In the north part of the State, no names of physicians are mentioned in history, or in the records of Providence prior to 1700. It appears by a letter of Roger Williams to his friend Winthrop, at New London, dated twelve years after the settlement of Providence, (1648, wherein he thanks him for sending some advice and medicines,) that in the sickness of himself and family, he depended on his own skill and on some medical books in his possession. The number of inhabitants at this time (1648) capable of bearing arms in the county of Providence was only about one hundred, and a population so small and isolated, could hardly increase to such an extent for many years, as to make it expedient to invite a physician, had there been one ready to settle among them; especially as there were eminent ones in Newport who could be brought by water in a few hours, and who needed all the patronage that both places afforded, for their support. In 1676 most of the inhabitants were driven from Providence and Seekonk, by Indians. In four or five years after, most of them had returned, and they employed, from that time, Dr. RICHARD BOWEN, of Seekonk, only two miles from Providence, who appears to have been the first settled physician there, and to have attended the sick of both places until about 1700.

About this time appears a practitioner of Providence, named HOYLE. He owned a large estate, probably including the site of Hoyle Tavern. He soon after gave an acre of land for the support of a Congregational church, near the present site of Richmond street church.

Soon after 1700, Dr. JABEZ BOWEN, the son of Dr. THOMAS, and grandson of Dr. RICHARD, of Seekonk, settled in Providence. As the name acquired great professional eminence, we will give a brief sketch of the Bowen family.

As early as 1680, Dr. RICHARD BOWEN, son of Dr. Thomas, and grandson of Richard, was engaged in medical practice in Seekonk, Mass., within two miles of Providence, whose sick he attended during more than twenty years, before it had any settled physician within its own limits. Dr. Richard educated two sons to the profession, THOMAS and JABEZ. JABEZ settled in Providence, on the home lot of Roger Williams, a few rods south of St. John's church, corner of North Main and Bowen streets. He had a son BENJAMIN, who succeeded him, and a grandson, Dr. JOSEPH, who died many years ago at an advanced age, in Glocester, R. I. Thomas Bowen, son of Dr. Richard and brother of Jabez, settled with his father in Seekonk. He had three sons, one of whom, named EPHRAIM, lived in Providence, with his uncle, Dr. Jabez, from the age of nine years, and finally studied medicine with him. He settled on the site of the Franklin House, where he died in 1812, aged 96 years. He had six sons, two of whom became physicians,—WILLIAM, who lived opposite his father's and practiced till 1832, when he deceased at the age of 86 years; and PARDON, who died in 1826, at an advanced age. These two, with their father, gained great celebrity.

Dr. WILLIAM BOWEN, the son of Dr. Ephraim, entered Harvard College, and, after one year, removed to Yale College, where he graduated in 1766. He studied with his father and attended lectures in Philadelphia. He was an extensive and successful practitioner, to the last year of his life, which terminated in 1832, at the age of 86. He was a polished gentlemen of the old school, of most affable and winning manners. He educated a large number of pupils, among whom were Drs. Wheaton, Fiske and Carpenter. He avoided surgical practice; but in diseases of women and children he excelled; and he was particularly skillful in the treatment of fevers, and a close observer of nature. He was a great sufferer from periodical gout, and often, in anticipation of an attack, would accelerate its onset, by wearing stiff cowhide boots. In the sick-room, his gentleness and suavity of manner won the hearts of his patients, and made him a most welcome visitor. His dress was a drab coat, vest and shorts, with yellow topped boots; his hair combed back and sometimes powdered, and curled on the temples, and a queue behind. He petitioned for the Charter, and was the second President of the Society.

PARDON BOWEN.—This accomplished physician and excellent man was born in Providence, 1757. He was the fifth son of Dr. Ephraim Bowen, whose valuable life, protracted to nearly a century, terminated in 1812. He graduated at Brown University in the year 1775. After the usual preparatory course of study under his brother, Dr. William Bowen, he, in the year 1779, embarked as the Surgeon of a privateer, fitted out for the destruction of British commerce. The ship was soon captured and carried into Halifax, where, during an imprisonment of seven months, he endured no common privations and suffering. After being regularly exchanged, he returned home; but soon after engaged in repeated enterprises of the kind, with similar results, until after a hard-fought battle of two hours, his vessel gained a signal victory over the enemy, and his prize money made some amends for his sufferings and privations.

Resolved to establish himself in his native town, he, in the year 1788, attended lectures in Philadelphia, and subsequently commenced practice in the various branches of his profession. His progress, though slow at first, gradually acquired speed, until he attained to the highest eminence, both as a physician and surgeon, in the State. His kind and conciliatory manner and warm-hearted benevolence, won the esteem and admiration of all persons.

Dr. Bowen contributed, occasionally, to the Medical Journals of the day, and in the fourth volume of Hosack's and Francis's Register, may be found an account from his pen, of the yellow fever as it prevailed in Providence, in the year 1805. Desirous to keep pace with the progress of the profession, he was diligent in reading those periodical publications which are calculated to keep one posted up in all that relates to discoveries and improvements.

Dr. Bowen was an active member of the Rhode Island Medical Society, and for seven years its presiding officer. He was also a Fellow of the American Antiquarian Society, and a member of the Board of Trustees of Brown University.

In the winter of 1820, the professional usefulness of this eminent and beloved physician was terminated by an attack of hemiplegia, which seized him without premonition, and threatened the immediate extinction of life. The worst fears of his friends were not, however, thus suddenly realized; he partially recovered the use of his limbs, and not long afterwards retired to the residence of his son-in-law, Franklin Greene, Esquire, Potowomut, (Warwick,) about fifteen miles from Providence. It was his favorite retreat from the toils of professional life, and was destined to receive his last sigh, in the bosom of an affectionate family, on the 25th of October, 1826; aged 69.

The above is chiefly abstracted from an obituary of Dr. Bowen, contained in Thatcher's Lives of Eminent Physicians, written by the late Professor Goddard, which concludes in the following just tribute to his memory:— "By his friends, he was a man indeed to be ardently loved, for they daily witnessed the benignity of his nature, the engaging suavity of his manners, the variety and richness and clear intelligence of his conversation, the generous expansion of his sensibilities, and the inflexible rectitude of his principles. The pressure of business never made him careless of the feelings and interests of others. Indeed, he was remarkable for that moral cultivation which respects the rights of all; and few showed a nicer discernment of the essential peculiarities which distinguish one being from another, and a more benevolent and delicate adjustment of all in every class. Notwithstanding his elevated reputation as a physician, and the opulence of his intellectual attainments, he was on all occasions a pattern of engaging modesty, seeking rather to support the happiness of others than to win their applause. Singularly exempt from that feverish thirst for distinction which is allayed by the cheap honors of society, he was happy in his walk of revered but unobtrusive usefulness, ministering to the comfort of his fellow creatures, when bereaved of health, or oppressed by poverty, or sinking in death. Though for nearly half a century engaged in the active discharge of professional duty, his heart retained its original purity, uncorrupted by an undue attachment to wealth or fame. His fortune was never ample, but the stream of his beneficence flowed with an equal and unchecked current. Such were some of the prominent characteristics of Dr. Pardon Bowen. He had high capacities, and he exerted them for the good of his kind. His life, in all its stages, was a beautiful exhibition of the virtues, and, at its close, an example of Christian holiness. His pure spirit, while on earth, took a wide and lofty range; and now that it has ascended to its Maker, the belief is not presumptuous, that it is gladdened by the joys of Heaven, and sublimed by the contemplations of immortality."

Dr. WILLIAM C. BOWEN, M. D., the only son of Dr. William Bowen, of Providence, was born June 2d, 1785. He entered Rhode Island College, but removed to Union College, in Schenectady, New York, with President Maxcy, at the time he accepted the presidency of that institution, and was graduated there in 1803. On his return to Providence, he commenced the study of medicine with his uncle, Dr. Pardon Bowen, with whom he continued till 1806, when he embarked for Europe to complete his education. He studied in Edinburg under the instructions of Professor Hamilton, and in 1807 received his degree, choosing for the subject of his inaugural dissertation, "De Sanguine Mittendo." He passed some months in Holland, one season in Paris, and went thence to London, and became the private pupil of Sir Astley Cooper, with whom he continued till August, 1811. He then returned to his native city, and commenced the practice of physic and surgery. In 1811, he was chosen Professor of Chemistry in Brown University, and delivered two courses of lectures. About this time, he commenced a course of experiments to discover the basis of the bleaching liquor which was just then brought into use in England. This he did, having in view the formation of a bleaching establishment in Providence. But the exposure of his lungs in this pursuit, to the action of noxious acids, laid the foundation of disease that proved fatal. He died April 23d, 1815, in the thirtieth year of his age.

In the death of Dr. William C. Bowen, Rhode Island lost its brightest ornament of the medical profession. No one before his time had enjoyed the privilege of sitting under the teachings of the first men in Europe, for so great a length of time; and, with his ardor in the pursuit of professional knowledge, he could not fail of attaining to great celebrity. His suavity and kindness of manner endeared him to all who were the subjects of his professional care; and no one could be more successful in gaining the respect and confidence of the good and the wise. In proof of this, it may be observed that his preceptor, Dr. Hamilton, of Edinburg, called him in consultation in a perilous disease of his own wife; and the writer of this notice had the satisfaction of hearing very honorable mention made of his talents by Sir Astley Cooper. His labors upon chlorine, though destructive to his own fortune and health and life, laid the foundation of the present flourishing bleacheries in Rhode Island, that have proved so conducive to its welfare and prosperity.

Dr. John Walton practiced medicine some years, and became a minister in the First Baptist Church about the year 1730.

Dr. Jonathan Randall died Octobor 17th, 1724, in his 36th year.

Drs. Ephraim Bowen, Joseph Hewes, Sen., and Jonathan Arnold were cotemporaries about the revolutionary period, and were the most eminent physicians of their day, in the county, if not in the State. Dr. Hewes lived in the street since named from him. I can gather only that he was considered a man of talents, and, for that day, well educated. He took pupils, among whom were Drs. Jonathan Arnold, Stephen Randall and Joseph Hewes, Jr. He was eccentric, and fond of jests and anecdotes. He died September 30th, 1796, aged 82.

Dr. Jonathan Arnold had charge of the Army Hospital, established in Providence during the early part of the revolutionary war, and acted as Purveyor of medical supplies. Some years after peace was restored, he was sent as a representative to Congress, which office his son, the late Lemuel H. Arnold, afterwards held. Dr. Arnold resided at the foot of Constitution Hill. He finally moved to the State of Vermont, where he died.

Dr. Joseph Hewes, Jr., died August, 1770, aged 32 years.

Stephen Randall was a pupil of Dr. Hewes, and practiced at the North end. He died March 15th, 1843, aged 81.

Dr. John Bass was first a clergyman in the present church of Rev. Dr. Hall.

Ephraim Comstock, son of Dr. Benjamin, of Smithfield, died of yellow fever, 1797, aged 37.

Dr. Amos Throop, whose name stands at the head of the list of Presidents of the Rhode Island Medical Society, was born in Woodstock, Conn., in the year 1738. He left home early in life, and came to Providence, poor and friendless, where he practiced medicine until his death, in April, 1814, at the age of 76 years. He is represented as kind to the poor, and indulgent, if not negligent, in the collection of his bills, even of the rich, most of whose bills remained to be collected after his decease; and it is known that one of his bills against a man was for his own delivery into the world. He was the first male accoucheur in Providence.

Soon after his arrival in Providence, he married Mary Bernon Crawford, and was mainly indebted to her skill and sagacity in the sale and purchase of drugs and medicines. Physicians, in his time, furnished their own medicines, and augmented their meagre charges for visits by a liberal profit on the doses they prescribed.

Foreseeing an interruption of the importations from England at the commencement of the revolution, the doctor's wife induced him to order an extraordinarily large invoice of drugs and medicines, from a London correspondent, to the utmost extent of his means of payment. To prevent disappointment by miscarriage of the order, a copy was dispatched by the next vessel, without the usual mercantile prefix of "*duplicate*." In due time a reply was received, advising of the shipment of both orders, to the dismay of the doctor. The seasonable arrival of such an extraordinary quantity of drugs and medicines at the commencement of the revolutionary war proved highly beneficial to the inhabitants of the colonies, and to the soldiers of the army, and also to the author of this fortunate mistake, in particular.

In personal appearance, Dr. Throop was tall, and of an erect, combined with a commanding deportment; and displayed the characteristics of "a gentleman of the old school." In accordance with the fashion of the day, he wore a powdered wig, with several stiff tiers of curls imported direct from London. It is narrated that the wig box was appropriated and used for a chopping-tray for force meat balls, by the French cook who served several officers of the French army, then quartered in the house of Dr. Throop.

During some period of the war, Dr. Throop volunteered to serve in a military company. Here he was selected to serve in the capacity of fugleman. He humorously described the shock which his military pride received at a review, when, in an attempt to shoulder his musket in an exemplary style, it fell to the ground simultaneously with his cocked hat and wig. He affirmed that he was ever afterwards content to confine his ambition to serving as a son of Esculapius instead of a son of Mars, and to display his skill in the use of blue pills instead of leaden ones.

Dr. Throop was elected a representative of the town of Providence, in the General Assembly of the State, during several sessions, and served as President of the Exchange Bank of this city, from its first establishment to the time of his death. He left no children, and his family name became extinct in Providence.

The following sketch of Dr. Wheaton's life is condensed from an elaborate discourse read before the Rhode Island Historical Society :—

Levi Wheaton was born in Providence, R. I., February 6th, 1761. He was the son of Deacon Ephraim Wheaton, and the fourth lineal descendant of Robert Wheaton, who emigrated from Wales, and settled in Rehoboth, Mass., about the year 1640. * * *

He entered Rhode Island College in 1774, but in consequence of the national disturbances of the times, his collegiate course was interrupted in 1776, and he did not graduate as A. B. till 1782. In the meantime, however, he had pursued his classical studies, and without any definite object in view, not having decided upon a profession, he read, during this period, some of the standard works upon medicine and surgery. He also, during this interruption of his regular course of studies, had an opportunity of seeing something of medical and surgical practice in the office of Dr. Hewes, a friend and neighbor. At the age of sixteen, he passed a season in the town of Smithfield, teaching school. In referring to this period of his life, in an autobiography, written some two or three years before his death, he says that he became familiar with Pope's works, at an early age; and after making some remarks upon that author, he adds:— "I record this especially as an *event* in my life, for, strange as it may seem, I think I can say with truth, no writer has had so much influence on my tone of thinking of men and things."

In the year 1778, he entered the Military Hospital in Providence, as a volunteer. The summer of 1779 he passed at Westerly, studying medicine with Dr. Babcock, and in the following year he completed his medical education under the tuition of Dr. William Bowen, of Providence. After finishing his medical education, he served as Surgeon on board a privateer; and in the autumn of 1782, while cruising off the southern coast, was taken prisoner and carried into New York, by the British frigate Vestal. While detained prisoner in New

York, he had charge, for some months, of the Prison Hospital Ship Falmouth; and ever afterwards this event was recalled with much pleasure, as having afforded him an opportunity of rendering some good offices to his imprisoned countrymen. After the close of the war, he accepted an invitation to settle in Hudson, N. Y., which was then being settled by eastern people. He remained in Hudson some ten years, during which time he not only practiced his profession with success, but was appointed to several public offices of trust and emolument. The settlement of Hudson, however, after a few years' experiment, proved a failure; the town declined as rapidly as it had grown, and the doctor becoming dissatisfied with his prospects, removed to New York city, where he spent two years, when the death of Dr. Comstock, who was doing a large business in Providence, seemed to make an opening for him, and he yielded to urgent solicitations of his friends, to return and permanently establish himself in his native town.

In the early part of his career in Providence, he, in connection with Dr. William Bowen, established a Small Pox Hospital, to which many resorted for inoculation.

When, in 1812, a Medical School was organized in Brown University, Dr. Wheaton was appointed Professor of the Theory and Practice of Physic; but the school not being well sustained, he did not at that time lecture. Dr. William Ingalls, of Boston, was appointed Professor of Anatomy and Surgery, and gave one or two courses of lectures upon those subjects at the University, and then transferred his lectures to Boston. When, however, in 1822, the Medical School was reörganized, Dr. Wheaton gave three or four courses of lectures upon the Theory and Practic of Physic and Obstetrics, which were very creditable to his talents.

Dr. Wheaton was for many years one of the corporation of Brown University, and, at the time of his decease, was at the head of the list of that honorable body. He was for many years Physician to the Marine Hospital at the port of Providence. This, besides affording him a small cash salary, enabled him to give his students, of whom he had many, advantages superior to those generally enjoyed in this locality.

As a practitioner, Dr. Wheaton was cautious, but not timid; and though inclined to conservatism, he did not hesitate to essay any new remedy when proposed by those in whose opinions he had confidence; or to adopt new views when emanating from a reliable source, and bearing the impress of plausibility; or, in other words, if he was cautious in admitting new doctrines and relying upon new remedies, he was not like one blind to the progress of the art.

His practice was based upon the theory, that diseases, in this climate at least, are generally inflammatory, and, that when inflammation is controlled, the disease subsides, as a necessary consequence; hence, venesection, tart. antimony, nit. potash, Epsom salts and calomel were among the remedies upon which he placed the greatest reliance. It was a common remark with him, "that we did not bleed enough; that there was no remedy of equal value in the treatment of our diseases." He has repeatedly told the writer, that he had not had occasion to regret bleeding, in more than two or three instances in the whole course of his practice; but that he had very frequently regretted the omission of it. Whatever views may be entertained upon this subject in this age of improvements, when the resources of the art are almost indefinitely multiplied; or whatever changes may have taken place in the essential characters of diseases requiring modifications in treatment, no one who practiced medicine thirty or forty years ago, will doubt the success that attended the practice of bleeding at that time, or, indeed, that it really was the most potent means then known of controlling morbid action. Emetics and cathartics he dispensed much more frequently, and in a greater number of diseases and conditions than are at the present time prescribed. Opium, in its various preparations, was, particularly in the latter part of his life, a favorite medicine; and, in common with many others, he extended the use of it to diseases and conditions in which it had previously been prescribed with great caution, if not deemed wholly inadmissible. Among the other narcotics, conium and hyoscyamus were those which he most frequently prescribed. Belladonna and stramonium he seldom used, and aconite, veratrium viride, cannabis indica and a multitude of other remedies, now so much in vogue, constituted no part of his materia medica.

It was his usual practice to make brief memoranda of his cases every night, in his day-book, in connection with his charges for services, to which he would occasionally refer, to refresh his memory. It was rarely, however, that he had occasion to make such a reference, and those who knew him will recollect how particularly and circumstantially he would relate a case of days, or even weeks' duration, from his unaided memory. Every symptom and every prescription would be recalled with the utmost exactness.

It was not only as the thoroughly read and sound practical physician, that Dr. Wheaton was entitled to preëminence; but he was still more so as a man of erudition and general scholarship. He was a fine classical scholar, and was, to an unusual extent, familiar with both ancient and modern literature, and ready and frequent in his quotations in conversation. He never, to the last day of his life, ceased to be a student; nor did he in the least lose his interest in the literature of the age. Few works of any pretentions, whether medical, scientific or literary, escaped his notice.

As a prose writer, he had but few superiors; and he sometimes amused himself and friends with a poetical production. In the latter part of his life he often expressed the regret, that he had not devoted a portion of his leisure time to the preparation of some work for publication,—a regret in which all who knew him must participate. He says upon this subject:— "I live to regret that I have wasted days and years, and midnight oil, in desultory reading, with little other object than present amusement, with a mind passive rather than active, my brain a thoroughfare for other men's thoughts without exacting toll. For the health of the mind, as well as the body, due attention should be paid, not only to the quality and quantity of food taken, but to the time and space allotted for digestion. The brain, as well as the stomach, may be overloaded. Selection and method are essential to both; not all minds are omnivorous, yet the majority of readers are blinded by the opposite conceit."

An article upon Yellow Fever, as it appeared in Providence, and another upon Calomel, were published many years ago in one of the Philadelphia Journals. In 1832, a somewhat lengthy and valuable article upon Asiatic Cholera, from his pen, was published in the city newspapers; and later in life he contributed several papers to the Boston Medical and Surgical Journal, over the signature of "Senex." All these contributions to the general stock of knowledge, however, were ephemeral in their nature,—were admired for a season and then forgotten, and are wholly inadequate testimonials of his real ability.

Dr. Wheaton, in his stature, was tall and erect; in his deportment, was dignified and graceful. In his intercourse with members of the profession he was courteous and honorable, and he was always ready to instruct and advise in a friendly manner, those who applied to him for counsel, whether upon professional or other subjects.

To omit to speak particularly of the qualities of his heart would be to leave the story but half told. It is the general opinion that the physician becomes hardened to scenes of suffering and death, and his heart callous to human misery. This opinion, it is to be hoped, is unfounded in fact; but however it may be as a general rule, it was not so in the case of the subject of this sketch. Whenever he had under his care a painful and critical case, he seemed to experience the most extreme solicitude. It would be the all engrossing subject of his thought and the topic of his conversation. The best authorities would be examined, and perchance a medical friend consulted. The writer has more than once seen him walking his room at a late hour at night, wholly absorbed in anxious thought upon some critical case, and this, too, when the death of his patient would not have materially affected his reputation or his interest. Upon this subject he has thus spoken for himself. He says:— "I have at present two patients for whom I feel much anxiety. It is one of the miseries of the medical man, to meet with cases he cannot cure, and of the issue of which he is at least very doubtful, and painfully to forebode the complicated sufferings of a bereaved family. How often, alas, has my heart been wrung in this way for the last fifty years, and yet I am still in the land of the living! It is, indeed, a painful responsibility to see ourselves looked up to as guardian angels, and feel our insufficiency,—our utter inability to save the victim of disease. As far as I can analyze my own feelings, they are for the most part disinterested; homo sum! but sometimes, and often, the thought will obtrude itself,—am I not defeated and disgraced? If my conscience assures me of good intentions, were those intentions medically good? Were they fairly fulfilled, or were there not errors? Quæ incuria fudit, or, after all, will public opinion support me? How will it affect my living, my reputation,—that fancied life in others breath? Ah, what a life is that of a physician!"

His death, which occurred August 29th, 1852, was sudden and painless. He had, for some time, had an anomalous and troublesome affection of the left arm, and it was his opinion that there was a metastasis of that affection to the heart. The night previous to his death, which occurred in the morning, he had the diarrhœa, but how much that had to do with severing the long-drawn and tapering thread of life is uncertain. He was fully aware, for an hour perhaps before he expired, that his end was fast approaching; but he manifested no alarm or concern. He seemed to contemplate his case in a professional point of view, and to consider it a phenomenon in pathology.

While his afflicted family were standing around his dying

bed, listening to catch the last accents of his feeble voice, and administering to his last earthly wants, he requested them to read the following appropriate and beautiful prayer from Burns: —

"O Thou unknown, Almighty Cause
Of all my hope and fear;
In Whose dread presence, ere an hour,
Perhaps I must appear;—
If I have wandered in those paths
Of life I ought to shun,
As something, loudly, in my breast,
Remonstrates I have done;
Thou know'st that Thou hast formed me
With passions wild and strong;
And list'ning to their witching voice
Has often led me wrong.
Where human weakness has come short,
Or frailty stept aside,
Do Thou, all good! for such Thou art,—
In shades of darkness hide.
Where, with intention, I have err'd,
No other plea I have,
But Thou art good; and goodness still
Delighteth to forgive."

This request having been complied with, he very shortly afterwards sank calmly and imperceptibly into the sleep of death.

Thus passed away from the busy scenes of life, a man who had, for an uncommonly long series of years, been a useful and efficient member of society, an affectionate husband, a kind and indulgent father, and a physician and scholar who has had but few superiors in any age or country.

[Dr. Capron.]

Solomon Drowne, M. D.—Solomon Drowne was born in Providence, R. I., on the 11th of March, 1753. He was a descendant of Leonard Drowne, who came from England about the year 1670, and settled near Portsmouth, N. H.: but in 1692, on account of the Indian wars, removed to Boston. His grandson, Solomon Drowne, the father of the subject of the present sketch, became a resident of Providence in 1730, and was a prominent and useful citizen of this place for over half a century. Dr. Drowne, the second of his three children, was from early youth inclined to a life of study. Graduating at Brown University, in the class of 1773, with the highest honors, he studied medicine, for a year, under Dr. William Bowen; and in the autumn of 1774, commenced attending lectures in the University of Pennsylvania, at which he received his medical degree.

While engaged in his professional studies, he took an active interest in the military affairs of his native city, preparing, as it was, for the revolutionary struggle; and assisted, himself, in throwing up the fortifications in the vicinity. At a later period, he entered the service of the United States, as surgeon's mate in the General Hospital, under Dr. John Morgan, Director General of the Hospitals, and was in New York at the time of its evacuation by the American troops; at Westchester, New Castle, and other places in the State of New York; and at Norwalk in Connecticut. In 1777, he was in the Rhode Island State Hospital, for seven months; he was then promoted to the rank of Surgeon in Col. Crary's regiment, and in August, 1778, was in Sullivan's Expedition upon Rhode Island. After this, he was stationed for a time at Bristol, and on the 3d of August, 1780, was appointed Surgeon to Lieut. Col. Atwell's regiment.

The war of the revolution being over, Dr. Drowne commenced the practice of medicine in Providence. In 1783, he was elected to the Board of Fellows of Brown University, and was for a time its secretary. Desirous of perfecting, as far as possible, his professional education, in 1784 he visited Europe. "Some of my friends," he writes, on his passage, "expressed surprise at my quitting my home, and exposing myself to the fatigues and many disagreeable circumstances incident to so long a voyage, charitably deeming me sufficiently qualified for the practice of my profession. For my own part, I confess a strong, persevering desire, with bold, adventurous hand, to unfurl the veil that conceals from me the charms of nature and art; to visit different nations, and view the living manners as they rise; to penetrate as much as possible the source of useful knowledge; and, especially, to accomplish myself in the divine art of healing. Why did the Grecian philosophers and physicians travel to Egypt, &c.? But why do I ask this question? Can any one sit down at home and reach the sublimer hights of science? No; the sage Seneca knew better, seventeen centuries ago, when he said 'Imperitum est animal homo, et sine magna experientia rerum, si circumscribatur natalis soli sui fine.'" After a stormy and tedious passage of sixty-one days, in the depth of winter, he reached London, and for several months attended the Hospitals of St. Bartholomew, St. Thomas, and Guy's, hearing lectures from Cline, Hunter, and others. While in England, he formed the acquaintance of Doctors Pole, Moreton, Lettsom, and Sharpe; also that of Mr. Granville Sharpe, Sheridan, and others, with many of whom he afterwards corresponded. In May, 1785, he crossed to the Hague, and after travelling over Holland and Belgium, proceeded to Paris. Here he attended the lectures of Pelleton, Louis, Brisson and others; and visited the various hospitals almost daily. During his stay in France, he became acquainted with several distinguished men of the time, whom he met at the table of Dr. Franklin, at whose house at Passy he was a frequent guest; and also at the residence of Gov. Jefferson, who soon after succeeded Franklin as our minister in Paris. His journal, during this period, contains a minute and lively description of all prominent places and objects of interest, particularly botanical gardens, rare plants, and works of art, for which he always cherished a partiality amounting to enthusiasm.

On his return to Providence, he resumed the practice of his profession; but shortly after, in 1788, journeyed to Ohio, and resided for nearly a year at Marietta, having become one of the proprietors of the Ohio Company. While in this place, he attended Gen. Varnum, then one of the judges in the

Northwestern Territory, in the illness of which he died; and, at the request of the Ohio Company, pronounced his funeral eulogy, January 13th, 1789. He was present at the first anniversary of the settlement of Marietta, April 7th, 1789, on which occasion he delivered an oration in reference to that event, which was published. Subsequently, he resumed his practice in Providence; but, in consequence of ill-health, removed again to the West in 1792, and settled for a time at Morgantown, Virginia. In the spring of 1794, the danger from the border incursions of the Indians being over, he proceeded to Union, Fayette county, Pennsylvania, where he resided seven years. Here he delivered four orations commemorative of American Independence, and also an eulogy on Gen. Washington, "in conformity to the proclamation of the President of the United States," February 22d, 1800, all of which were published at the time, and were distinguished for their classical elegance and patriotic spirit.

Dr. Drowne retraced his steps to Rhode Island, in 1801, and soon afterwards settled in the town of Foster, purchasing an estate adjoining that of his friend, the Hon. Theodore Foster, for many years a senator in Congress, who expected, ere long, to withdraw from public life and become his permanent neighbor. He was led to select this spot, from several considerations. He was exceedingly fond of rural life, and a close student and warm admirer of nature. The varied character of the scenery here, diversified as it is by thrifty groves, abrupt hills, and frequent streams; the high elevation, so favorable to health and longevity; and the perfect retirement, so congenial to his tastes, and well adapted for literary and botanical pursuits, made this sylvan retreat peculiarly attractive to him. In allusion to its healthfulness, he called it Mount Hygeia, a name which it still bears. Here he built a spacious residence, and settled down for the remainder of his days, devoting himself to his professional engagements, to agriculture, and to elegant letters. His first care was to adorn his grounds with a great variety of ornamental and fruit trees, obtained from different parts of the country; and to arrange a botanical garden, which, in a few years, for its size, rare and beautiful plants, and careful cultivation, as well as from the circumstance that it was the first garden of the kind in the State, acquired a wide notoriety, and was visited from far and near. From his professional tours, which extended to Providence, and not unfrequently to other States, he always returned with seeds or plants to enrich his collection. He also sent abroad for plants, and was the first to introduce many new species into our country, which have since become common. In his greenhouse of exotics, and his extensive garden grounds filled with countless varieties of indigenous and acclimated plants, where he daily walked to enjoy the scene, to give directions for their proper culture, or for the purpose of scientific study; with his extensive library, of which a large portion was in the French language, and of the greatest value in medicine and botany; and more than all, in the society of his wife and children, who had imbibed his tastes and participated in his studies; and in the society of cultivated friends visiting him, Dr. Drowne gave himself up to unalloyed enjoyment during the intervals which he could pass at home.

In 1811, Dr. Drowne was appointed Professor of Materia Medica and Botany in Brown University, and delivered courses of lectures in that institution until a few years before his death, and occasionally, also, to private classes in Providence and other cities. "His attention to Botany," says a brother physician in a published sketch of his life, "was directed not more to the philosophy of the science than to its practical uses in agriculture and medicine. It may truly be said, that no individual in this State has equalled him in these practical applications. * * As a popular lecturer on Botany, Dr. Drowne has probably never been equalled in this country. His various knowledge, fine classical taste, and lively imagination, eminently qualified him to illustrate and embellish the science of which he was an enamoured votary from early youth." Under his direction, the students of Brown University began, upon the college grounds, a botanical garden, which, had it been kept up to the present time, would not only have contributed to the health and mental recreation of the undergraduates, and assisted them in their studies of vegetable physiology and chemistry, but would have largely promoted the arts of floriculture, horticulture, and agriculture throughout the State.

The Rhode Island Medical Society, of which Dr. Drowne was vice-president, appointed him a delegate to the Convention that formed the National Pharmacopœia in 1819. A few years later, at the oft-repeated request of the Society, he gave the annual address,—a performance which furnishes an accurate index to his professional opinions and practice. "Were I to prefix a text to my brief, desultory discourse," he said, "it would be '*In simplici, salus;*'—restoration to health depends on simplicity in remedies; or, more literally, there is safety in simple things. What a farrago of drugs has been, and perhaps still is, used by many physicians. 'I have really seen in private practice, and in some public writings,' says Huxham, 'such a jumble of things thrown together in one prescription, that it would have puzzled Apollo himself to know what it was designed for.' A practitioner in the country said that the quantity, or rather complexity, of the medicines which he gave his patients, was always increased in a ratio with the obscurity of the cases; 'if,' said he, 'I fire a great profusion of shot, it is very extraordinary if some do not hit the mark.' A patient in the hands of such a practitioner has not a much better chance than the Chinese mandarin, who, upon being attacked with any disease, calls in twelve or more physicians, and then swallows, in one mixture, all the potions which each separately prescribes. Bewildered by thorny theories, unstable as the phases of the moon, it would be far better for the practitioner to tread the path pointed out by a strict observance of nature. * * On a review of my own practice, I think I have perceived greater advantages from the use of simple indigenous remedies, than of others commonly prescribed. * * It is to the simplicity and paucity of remedies used,—to attention to the *natural habit* and regimen, that I can, with least hesitancy, ascribe my success in practice. By this I would not be understood to boast of cures performed; those were effected by the work of nature. What can we do more than merely to regulate the *vis medicatrix naturæ*, the self-preserving energy, by exciting it when languid, restraining it when vehement, in changing morbid action, or in obviating pain or irritation, when they oppose its salutary courses?" The change which has gradually come over the medical practice in this regard, since his day, shows the wisdom and foresight of the principles which he advocated. And it cannot be doubted that, to his patient observation of the natural habit of his patients, and the use of mild medicines, his great eminence in chronic diseases, and with constitutions enfeebled almost beyond the relief of ordinary remedies, is mainly to be attributed.

Dr. Drowne was deeply interested in the Rhode Island Society for the Encouragement of Domestic Industry, in the organization and proceedings of which he took an active part: and on October 15th, 1823, and on several subsequent occasions, he delivered the annual addresses. These contain many original and valuable practical suggestions; and, no doubt, tended to excite in the minds of all who heard or read them, a spirit of enterprise and emulation for an intelligent cultivation of the soil, for ornamental gardening with its enchanting scenery, and for whatever could add to the attractiveness and comfort of their rural abodes. His last address, delivered on September 23d, 1833, when he was over eighty years old, treats of the great benefits to be derived from the combined Agricultural, Classical and Mechanical School at Pawtuxet, in the establishment of which, under the auspices of the Agricultural Society, he had long been a warm advocate. He earnestly recommends to the founders and students of the institution, to lay out a botanical garden, for the introduction and trial of all foreign and other plants, which might prove worthy of general cultivation; for testing the qualities of soils, rotation of crops, &c.; and thus to ascertain important facts, and publish them for the public benefit. It was his often expressed opinion throughout life, that the most useful, honorable, and independent occupation in the world was that of the husbandman. "Health, acuteness of intellect, and contentment,—heaven's choicest blessings," he was wont to say, "spring from such excellent exercise."

In 1824, he published the "Compendium of Agriculture, or the Farmer's Guide in the most essential parts of Husbandry and Gardening," a treatise of which it was justly remarked, that, "it would be difficult, in the same number of words, to comprise a greater number of ideas which may prove practically important to the agriculturist."

At the earnest request of the citizens of Providence, Dr. Drowne delivered before them, on February 23d, 1824, an "Oration in Aid of the Cause of the Greeks," whose unequal struggle with the Turks was at that time calling forth the sympathy and assistance of this country. Towards the close of this able and highly finished oration, after eloquently portraying the inhuman barbarities which the inhabitants of Cyprus and Scio were suffering, and when his fervid manner had somewhat wearied his strength and lowered the tones of his voice, already tremulous with age, he introduces the following happy allusions to himself:— "There is a sort of magic in the name of Greece. Often, in fancy, have I roamed about the classic fields and groves of that felicitous region, transported by a thousand agreeable associations. 'Tis true, Parnassus' dizzy hight I dared not climb. It fitted better to haunt Boeotian shades, and listen to the wood-notes sweet of Hesiod, when he sung the rural cares of Grecian husbandmen. Or, to ramble with Theophrastus, and gather interesting plants upon the Lesbian hills, or the delightful slopes of Mount Hymettus, or where

'Elissus rolls his whisp'ring streams.'

* * O Greece! thou wert the cradle of all that is elegant in art; of all that is fascinating in poetry and literature; of all that is excellent in legislative and political science, or splendid in martial achievements; of all, in a word, that can add interest and true nobility to the human character. Thy mighty genius has slumbered for many ages; but it is now awakening from a long night of melancholy stupor, and shedding gleams of glory round thee, emulative of that which adorned thee in the zenith of thy former splendor. We, though far remote, and separated from thee by the multitudinous waves of ocean and the midland sea, yet cannot look with frigid indifference upon thy virtuous struggles, for all that mankind hold most dear. There are still some remaining among us, who have participated in like conflicts, for the ennobling prize of Liberty! Ancient nursery of Freedom — Greece! — farewell: but we bid the not *farewell,* without an effort to *assist thee.*"

"The effect of this touching appeal," writes one who was present, "was hightened by the circumstances of the occasion. The thrilling tones of a heavy choir, chanting —

'Sound the loud trump o'er the Ægean sea;
The Moslem has fallen, and Greece shall be free!'—

the reverential aspect of an aged clergyman, earnestly invoking Heaven's interposition in behalf of a bleeding people,— and the venerable head of the orator, bowed with years, and white as the snow through whose chilling depths he had waded to plead their cause before an assembled multitude, with such fervor and pathos,—gave to the scene an air of moral sublimity, rarely equalled."

Dr. Drowne departed this life on February 5th, 1834, after a brief illness, at the advanced age of eighty-one years; and was buried on an eminence near his residence, overlooking the orchard and garden grounds, and under the shade of his favorite robinias. His wife, Elizabeth Russell, of Boston, whom he married November 20th, 1777, survived him several years, dying May 15th, 1844, in her eighty-sixth year.

In stature, Dr. Drowne was a little lower than the common hight; in his manners and conversation, polished and engaging; and while exceedingly fond of cultivated society, at the same time fond of retirement. He was inclined to abstraction, and often, in visiting his patients, has been known, when his attention has been arrested by botanical objects, to become so absorbed in his favorite science as to cause serious delay. His love of nature was always an absorbing passion. The ancient Greek and Roman classics, and English poetry and literature generally, were his constant delight. During his whole life, he was a careful and laborious reader of books, and when interested in a volume was usually retained for hours in a standing posture; and having a retentive memory, he amassed an inexhaustible fund of useful and interesting information on all subjects, which, with his amiable and courteous bearing, made him a most welcome guest wherever he went. His public orations and addresses are highly creditable to him as a man of refined taste and varied acquisitions; while his delivery was noted for its natural grace and impassioned eloquence.

Dr. Drowne was a member of the American Academy of Arts and Sciences, and an honorary member of several other learned bodies. He was extensively known, by reputation, to the medical profession throughout the United States and abroad. A few years before his death, he prepared, by request, an account of the climate, mineral springs, medicinal substances, diseases and mode of treatment, &c., of his native State, for the Royal College of Physicians in London. He carried on an extensive correspondence with many eminent medical and scientific men in Europe and America. Besides the publications already noticed, he contributed numerous articles to newspapers and scientific journals; and left, in manuscript, several occasional addresses, a number of journals of tours in this country and Europe, and an extensive course of lectures on Botany and Materia Medica.

*East Greenwich.*—Dr. DUTEE JERAULD settled in East Greenwich, in the year 1742. He was a native of Medfield, Mass. His parents were French. His father was a physician. After residing in this town four or five years, he removed into Warwick, on the road to Apponaug, at a point about equi-distant between the two villages. The house in which he lived is now owned by the town, and used as an asylum for the poor. He died in July, 1813, at the advanced age of 91 years.

From all that can be learned, at this date, of the character of Dr. Jerauld, he must have been a worthy and estimable man. For many years after his death, his memory was fondly cherished by a large circle of friends and patients; and many anecdotes and incidents of his life are still told, which plainly show the genial humor and benevolent spirit of his character.

As a physician, his mode of practice never, at any time, approached the heroic order; and in the latter period of his life, when his business was chiefly confined to chronic diseases, it was extremely mild and simple, and if it was inefficacious, had the merit of doing no harm,—his kind manner and encouraging words doing more towards the cure or comfort of his patients than the roots and herbs, of which his prescriptions mainly consisted.

Dr. PETER TURNER came to East Greenwich and established himself as a physician and surgeon, in 1782. Dr. Turner was the son of Dr. William Turner, of Newark, New Jersey, and the grandson of Captain William Turner, of Newport, Rhode Island. He was born September 2d, 1751; married, in 1776, the daughter of Cromwell Childs, of Warren, and died in East Greenwich, February 14th, 1822. Of his early life, I have been able to learn but little. His father died when he was very young, and left him in the care of his half-brother, Dr. Canfield, with whom he studied medicine. At the breaking out of the revolution, he joined the army, and was attached to one of the Rhode Island regiments, (Col. Greene's,) as Surgeon, and served through the whole war.

He was induced to settle in this town, from the fact that he had formed many acquaintances here, in the army; and also, from the circumstance that Gen. Varnum, who was his brother-in law, resided here, at that time.

Dr. Turner was the first Surgeon who had ever practiced in this part of the State. Coming from the army, the good people of the neighboring country looked upon him with no little distrust, fearing that he might take off an arm or a leg, without even so much as saying, "by your leave." But this feeling of apprehension soon wore off, and he was engaged in a very large practice, extending ten miles, or more, in every direction. He was considered a skillful Surgeon, and a bold and successful operator; and from all accounts, he much preferred this department of his calling to the practice of medicine. As a physician, he pursued, as a general rule, a routine system, strictly following the injunctions he had received from authority, in early life, and looking with but little favor upon any innovation or improvement which trespassed upon acknowledged doctrine; and if some of the novelties of our own time had existed in his day, they would have met with decided opposition and disapprobation.

In his figure and personal appearance, Dr. Turner was short and rather fleshy. He had lost the sight of one eye, over which he wore a green patch, or shaded it with his hand, as he walked in the streets. He was very active and quick in all his movements; social in his habits; fond of conversation and anecdote, and no man could tell a story with a better grace.

Dr. Turner had, at different times, many students, some of them afterwards our most respectable physicians. The late Dr. William Turner, of Newport, who was his nephew and son-in-law, finished his course of study in his office. The late Dr. Tibbitts, of Apponaug, was a pupil of his, and Dr. Thomas Tillinghast, who resided in the southwest part of the town of East Greenwich, and had a limited practice, devoting a part of his time to religious duties, as a preacher; and, also, his sons, Daniel,—who removed to St. Mary's, Georgia, and died of yellow fever; Henry, who left the profession and went to the west and afterwards to the south, where he is now living; and the present Dr. James V. Turner, of Newport.

For several years previous to his death, Dr. Turner was confined to his room, and for a great part of the time, rendered entirely helpless by a paralysis. He died February 14th, 1822, and was buried with Masonic honors, in a spot of his own selection, a short distance from his residence; but within a few years, his remains have been removed to Newport, and deposited in the family burying-ground.

Charles Eldredge, M. D., was born in Brooklyn, Conn., 1784. His father, James Eldredge, Esq., a native of Stonington, and at the commencement of the revolutionary war, he was a merchant. He joined the army and served as a captain, and in the commissary department. At the close of the war, he removed to Brooklyn and purchased an estate on the banks of the Quinnebaug, where he raised thirteen children, Charles being the ninth. Having improved his opportunities for a preparatory education for medicine, he spent two years in teaching school, and then became a pupil of Dr. Thomas Hubbard, of Pomfret. He then attended lectures in Philadelphia, and returning to Pomfret, he assisted his preceptor for some months, and then settled in East Greenwich, in 1810. He was soon engaged in extensive practice, not only in Greenwich, but also in the neighboring towns.

He was active and public spirited in the affairs of the town, its busines and its institutions of religion and learning, and a liberal contributor to its welfare, aud took a deep interest in the public affairs of the State. In 1826, he was elected to the senate of the State, and reëlected four successive years.

Reared on a farm, and spending much of his time in his early years in its cultivation, he always retained a fondness for agriculture, and, by precept and example, did much towards introducing improvements.

To the unfortunate and afflicted, he was ever ready with his sympathy and substantial aid. A terror to truant boys and vagabond men, he often took upon himself their guardianship, and succeeded in improving and informing them.

Although he could find opportunity to concern himself in the affairs of the town, by far the largest share of his time and thoughts were absorbed in professional duties. Commencing business when a malignant epidemic was raging over this part of New England, his practice became arduous and trying.

A disciple of Rush, his treatment of disease was marked by the peculiarities which the teachings of that distinguished man had given, and excited the criticisms of the neighboring physicians, and severe remarks from some of the most intelligent inhabitants of the town. His decided, consistent and honorable course of conduct soon gained for him the respect of one and the confidence and esteem of the other. The character of Dr. Rush he always held in the highest estimation, and professed himself the follower of his school of medicine; but probably he was much more indebted to himself than to any school or theory, for his success. His habits and power of observation, his quick perception and clear judgment enabled him to notice and to apprêciate every shade and variety which disease assumed. The epidemic tendency and influence of the season,—the peculiar constitution and idiosyncrasy of the patient, were always his careful study, and his prescriptions and treatment were adapted to their circumstances. Never hesitating to use potent means when the urgency of the case demanded, it was not his practice to give frequent doses to satisfy the whim of the patient, or to keep up appearances among the friends. His materia medica was simple, relying more upon well timed and efficient blows, than upon oft repeated and random shots. Without pretensions to remarkable literary acquirements, he kept himself well informed in the progress of medical science, and everything new in the way of improvement which his judgment and his experience could approve, he readily adopted.

For the practice of surgery, he was physically and mentally well fitted, and although he did not devote himself to it specially, his extensive reputation and acquaintance called him to all critical cases happening within a circuit of many miles. It was his pride to avoid rather than to perform heroic operations, and many times I have heard him speak with much satisfaction of the limbs he had saved after those frightful lacerations and fractures which so often happen in our cotton mills.

For the medical profession, he always manifested the liveliest interest. He was one of the petitioners for the charter of the Rhode Island Medical Society, and among its earliest members. In 1834, he was chosen President, and continued to hold the office for three years. He was an honorary member of the Connecticut Medical Society, and in 1835, received the degree of M. D. from Yale College.

In the winter of 1837–8, his pecuniary affairs became embarrassed. Previous to this time he had always been in easy circumstances, his income being amply sufficient for his own requirements, and allowing him to be liberal in his aid to others. He had now become hopelessly involved with a bankrupt manufacturing company, of which he was almost the only responsible member, and his property was insufficient to discharge the debt. Harrassed by this sudden and unexpected change in his affairs, a latent organic disease of the heart began to manifest itself, and his robust constitution, which had withstood the wear and tear of thirty years' hard service, began to show evident symptoms of decay. He soon became aware of the nature of the disease and its fatal tendency, and submitted with christian resignation and philosophic fortitude to the decrees of Providence. At times, his sufferings were very severe, but he continued to visit patients occasionally, until a short time before his death, which took place on the 15th day of September, 1838, in the fifty-fifth year of his age.

In his figure and personal appearance, Dr. Eldredge was tall and stoutly built, of a robust constitution, florid complexion and blue eyes. He possessed, in a marked degree, the virtue of hospitality; was fond of society and agreeable in conversation, and his manner was eminently fitted to inspire among the sick, hope and confidence.

In *Tiverton*, Drs. William Whittridge, a Vice President, William C. Whittridge, Richard M. Webber, Dennis Cook, Samuel West, M. D., first Vice President of the Society.

In *Little Compton*, Dr. Benjamin Richmond, who practiced during the revolution, and Dr. Almy, who succeeded him.

In *South Kingstown*, there have been several physicians of various degrees of eminence, viz.: — Drs. Charles Higginbottom, Sylvester, Robert and George Hazzard, William Chace, Joseph Torrey, Benjamin Waite, Joshua Perry, Ezekiel and John L. Comstock, and John Aldrich.

In *North Kingstown*, Drs. Gilbert Updike, John Parish, Jonathan Hazzard and Samuel Watson.

In *Charlestown*, Drs. Glazier, Mason, Bartlett, Newman, Stephen F. Griffen.

In *Westerly*, Drs. Blodget, Babcock, Dorrance, Vincent, Lea and Robinson.

In *Hopkinton*, Drs. Drake, Thomas and William Wilbour, Amos and Isaac Collins, and George W. Perry.

In *Warwick*, Drs. Samuel Hudson, Stephen Harris, John W. Tibbets, Sylvester Knight, Silas James, and Benjamin Nichols.

In *Cranston*, Drs. Comfort A. Carpenter, George W. Tyler, Robert Weeks, Daniel Baker, Jesse W. Olney, T. Aldrich, and Dr. Waterman.

In *Scituate*, Drs. Caleb Fiske, M. D., to be noticed hereafter, John Wilkinson, Jere Cole, Benjamin Slack, and John Anthony.

Caleb Fiske, M. D., deserves to be held in grateful remembrance, as a former President and a lasting benefactor to this Society. He was son of John Fiske, and a lineal descendant of Roger Williams, and was born in Scituate, R. I., close to the boundary of Cranston, about 105 years ago. He studied his profession with the late Dr. William Bowen; was a Surgeon in the army of the revolution, and served in that capacity at the time of General Sullivan's expedition against the British, on Rhode Island. He resided through most of his long life, at the place of his birth, where he died. At one time he was elected Judge of the Court of Common Pleas. He was one of the original members of this Society, named in its act of incorporation; and, in the year 1823, he succeeded Dr. Pardon Bowen, as its President. In 1821, he received an honorary degree of Doctor of Medicine, from Brown University. In addition to the cares of an extensive practice, he had a large number of medical students, among whom may be named the late Drs. Niles Manchester, of Pawtucket, and Daniel Baker, of Cranston; Dr. Harding Harris, and the following gentlemen, Drs. Rowland Greene, of Cranston, Stephen Harris, of Providence, and Daniel Green, of East Greenwich. Dr. Fiske died September, 1835, in the eighty-second year of his age, being then the oldest practicing physician in the State. He had accumulated a large property, and has left many highly respected descendants.

Dr. Fiske has perpetuated his name in connection with medical science, by his noble bequest, known as the Fiske Fund. The original bequest was forty shares in bank, of the par value of $2000, which, by subsequent accumulations, is now double that sum. A large number of dissertations, written for these premiums, have been published, and the Trustees of the Fund now offer two premiums of $100 each. The doctor also gave the Society a large portion of his Medical Library.

In *Foster,* SOLOMON DROWNE, M. D., already noticed at length, by his grandson, Rev. Mr. Drowne, of Brooklyn, N. Y.

In *Glocester,* Drs. JOSEPH BOWEN, ALLEN POTTER, ELEAZER BELLOWS. AARON WALDRON, HAZAEL POTTER and AUGUSTUS TORREY.

*Burrillville,* Dr. ELEAZER BELLOWS, Jr.

In *Smithfield,* Drs. BENJAMIN and ICHABOD COMSTOCK WILLIAM ARNOLD, J. SMITH, SIMEON BROWN, WILLIAM BUSHEE, who practiced before the revolution. After that period, and before the century closed, there were Drs. HARRINGTON, BALCOM, BAXTER and BENJAMIN COMSTOCK.

*North Providence,* Dr. NILES MANCHESTER, a Vice President.

In *Exeter,* Drs. SPRAGUE, TRIPP and MOORE.

In *Richmond,* Drs. HARRINGTON, AINSWORTH and PETISSA.

In *West Greenwich,* Dr. STEPHEN ALLEN.

In *Coventry,* Drs. CYREL CARPENTER and THOMAS O. H. CARPENTER. The latter was two years a medical officer of the navy in the Tripolitan war. He was remarkably eccentric.

In *Johnston,* Drs. MOSES MOWRY, STEPHEN, and his son, JEREMIAH WILCOX.

In *Cumberland,* Drs. EPHRAIM KNAPP, ABRAHAM MASON, NEHEMIAH A. POTTER, HALSEY D. and MICAH WALCOTT.

In *Bristol,* Hon. WILLIAM BRADFORD, of whom more will be said hereafter; also, Drs. BOURNE, GUSTAVUS BAYLIES, THOMAS NELSON, THOMAS WARREN, C. FOSTER, CALEB MILLER and LEMUEL W. BRIGGS.

The Hon. WILLIAM BRADFORD, just mentioned, was a descendant, in the fourth generation, from the Hon. William Bradford, second governor of Plymouth. He was born in Plympton, in the county of Plymouth. The natural bias of his mind led him to the study of medicine, and to this end he sought the instruction of Dr. Ezekiel Hersey, of Hingham, the generous benefactor of Harvard College. At the age of twenty-two, he commenced the practice of medicine, in the town of Warren, and soon gained a high reputation, particularly as an operative surgeon. After a few years, he removed to Bristol, where he not long after erected an elegant seat at Mount Hope.

After residing some years in Bristol, he entered upon the study of the law, partly from a love of juridical science, but more to find increase of employment and usefulness. His merits soon raised him to eminence, as a lawyer and politician. He was a leading member of the committee of correspondence, when the revolutionary struggle commenced, and a pillar of the cause. During the cannonade of Bristol, in the evening of October 7th, 1775, by the ships Rose, Glasgow and Syren, Governor Bradford went on board the Rose, in behalf of the inhabitants, and treated with Captain Wallace for the cessation of the bombardment. His own house was destroyed in the conflagration.

In 1792, he was elected a senator to Congress. Preferring a retired life, he soon resigned his seat for the delightful shades of his favorite retreat at Mount Hope. He held various offices, both State and municipal, and was, for many years, Deputy Governor and speaker of the General Assembly.

His industry and economy brought him an independent fortune, which he liberally shared with the poor; and it was his practice, for many years, to deposit with the clergyman of the parish, a liberal sum, to be distributed at the discretion of the minister.

He was an early riser; was temperate and moderate in his enjoyments, and retired early to his couch, which tended to prolong his life and activity to the age of fourscore. The last thirty years of his life he remained single, which time he cheered his solitary hours by the liberal entertainment of associates and strangers. He died July 6th, 1808. His eldest son, William Bradford, was aid to General Charles Lee, of the army.

In *Warren*, besides the Gov. Bradford just named, who resided there some years before he went to Bristol, there was a Dr. WILLIAM THOMPSON, ISAAC BARRUS, and his brother, DANIEL BARRUS, and JERE WILLIAMS, M. D., a Vice President of the Society.

The physicians of *Providence*, already noticed, with the exception of Dr. William C. Bowen, flourished prior to 1800. His name was inserted among them, in order that the Bowen family might come together.

There were other practitioners of Providence, of less note, prior to the above date, whom it is proper to mention, viz.:—Drs. THOMAS TRUEMAN, son of Jonathan T., who died in 1787, aged 35; Dr. HENRY STERLING, senior, died 1810, aged 83; HENRY STERLING, Jr., died 1800, aged 33; SOLOMON BRADFORD, died 1795, age 69; ROBERT GIBBS, died 1769, aged 73; JOHN SPURR, an Englishman, died 1810; JOSEPH MASON commenced practice 1780, and at one period sustained a respectable position in the profession; THOMAS GREENE was in good practice until his mind became impaired. But most of the above dealt in medicines, and attended chiefly to office calls, as did also Drs. STEPHEN RANDALL and BENJAMIN DYER.

After the commencement of the present century, several physicians of eminence entered upon the duties of the profession in Providence, and acquired distinguished reputation. They were highly educated, active and successful; were petitioners for the charter of the Rhode Island Medical Society, and strict observers of its rules and regulations. Their names were, JOHN M'KIE, M. D., JOHN M. EDDY, M. D., JACOB FULLER, M. D., THOMAS M. BARROWS, M. D., and PARDON BROWNELL,

M. D. They were cut down in the midst of their usefulness, which should serve to remind us of the uncertain tenure of our own lives. It is hoped that a more competent pen will, ere long, portray their professional career, and do justice to their merits. For reasons stated in our introduction, we decline undertaking the task.

Dr. WILLIAM TURNER, of *Newport,* was born at Newark, New Jersey, on the 10th of September, 1775, and was the son of Daniel Turner, and grandson of Dr. William Turner, of Newark, who was born in Newport, R. I., and was a pupil of Dr. Vigneron of that place.

Early in life, he entered the office of Dr. Jabez Campfield, of Morristown, New Jersey, as a student of medicine, and at the expiration of his pupilage, was examined and licensed to practice, and was admitted a Fellow of the Medical Society of that State. He soon after removed to East Greenwich, in this State, and entered into partnership with his uncle, Dr. Peter Turner, formerly a Surgeon in the revolutionary army, and for many years a leading practitioner in that town, and whose daughter he subsequently married. His health having declined, it was deemed advisable for him to try the effect of a sea voyage to a tropical climate, to which end, he applied for and obtained a commission, as Assistant Surgeon in the navy, dated August 31st, 1799. He cruised in the General Greene, among the West India islands, and on her return, his health being established, he settled in Newport, where he practiced with distinguished success, maintaining the first rank as an operative surgeon, in the south counties of this State, and was exceeded by none as a general practitioner, of high attainments and extensive popularity.

In September, 1812, he received a commission as Surgeon's mate in the army, and during the remainder of his life, gave daily attendance to the soldiers stationed at Fort Adams, in Newport. He declined promotion to a full Surgeon, knowing that its effect would be to remove him from his practice and comfortable home. He died suddenly, on the 26th of September, 1837, at the bedside of an obstetrical patient, being just sixty-two years of age.

As an operator and dresser, Dr. Turner was remarkable for neatness and dexterity, and would lead a spectator to believe that he had been trained in European hospitals. His judgment was clear and correct; his conversational powers of a high order, and remarkable for logical precision and elegant language. In the sick-room, he commanded great reverence and esteem, and his amiability of temper and amenity of manner won the affections of a wide circle of friends, which were exhibited in a striking degree by the vast concourse of citizens who assembled at his funeral, to weep over and lament their loss. He contributed but few papers to medical journals, and though an elegant writer, he was not fond of appearing before the public.

Dr. Turner had three brothers, all of them, as well as himself, officers in the navy, though his own term of service was only one voyage in the General Greene. The oldest brother, Benjamin, after serving some years, fell in a duel, fought with a son of Dr. Rush, of Philadelphia, who soon after lost his reason, remaining a maniac for life, in consequence, as is supposed, of this unhappy affair. The youngest brother, Henry E. Turner, entered the navy as a midshipman, in 1814, and died in 1820. He was a young officer of high promise, much beloved, and his early death greatly lamented by his brother officers, as well as by a heart stricken family.

Commodore Daniel Turner was intermediate in years, between the two last, and was a gallant officer, trained under Commodore Rodgers. He commanded the third ship in the battle of Lake Erie, being at the time only twenty-one years of age. His seamanship, and that of Sailing Master Taylor and Lieut. Holdup was exercised and thoroughly tested in rigging and outfitting the fleet on the lake. Of his conduct in the battle, Commodore Perry says:— "Lieutenant Turner, commanding the Caledonia, brought that vessel into action in the most able manner, and is an officer that, in all situations, may be relied on." In his later years he commanded the Pacific Squadron.

I have connected these names of Dr. Turner, in their present relation, from their having been his proteges and wards. He left a son, now Captain Peter Turner, the last survivor of the long list of navy officers furnished by that family.

EDMUND THOMAS WARING.—Doctor E. T. Waring was the fifth son of Thomas Waring, a planter of South Carolina. He was born in Charleston, S. C., December 25th, 1779. Having acquired the rudiments of learning, in the primary schools of his native city, he became a private pupil of the Rev. William Stoughton, D. D., a Baptist minister, then a resident of Georgetown, S. C., and afterwards the eloquent pastor of the Sansom Street Church, Philadelphia. A warm and abiding friendship between himself and his instructor affords a pleasing testimony to his diligence, his docility, and his progress in learning. From Georgetown he went to Providence, R. I., and pursued his studies privately, under the direction of the Rev. Jonathan Maxcy, D. D., the President of what was then Rhode Island College, and is now Brown University. Although he was not graduated at that institution, he enjoyed there those literary influences which always gather around a seat of sound learning, and was intimately acquainted with some who became distinguished among its alumni. Some of his academic contemporaries were Tristam Burges, David King, sen., Benjamin Shurtleff and Benjamin Renneau Simons, — the latter of whom was his medical attendant in his last illness. The class to which these gentlemen belonged was graduated in 1796.

From Providence, Mr. Waring removed to Newport, to pursue the study of medicine with Dr. Isaac Senter. From him he won the same regard and esteem which he had gained from his former teachers Soon after Dr. Senter's death, in 1779, he visited his native State, but soon returned to Newport, with a view of connecting himself, as a medical practitioner, with the son of his professional instructor. This project was not realized. He, however, continued for a while to serve the family of his late friend, and was long treated by them as a son. Having opened an office for himself, he soon, by his acknowledged skill, peculiar courtesy and polished manners, acquired an extensive practice, especially among his fellow Southerners, who already began to make Newport a favorite summer resort.

In 1803, Dr. Waring was married to Sophia F., daughter of Hon. Francis Malbone, United States Senator from Rhode Island. Ten children, all born in Newport, were the fruit of this marriage. Mrs. Waring died in 1823, in giving birth to the tenth.

For more than thirty years, Dr. Waring practiced medicine in Newport, respected by his fellow citizens, and successful in the performance of the duties of his profession. During nearly all of this period, he was the Physician of the United States Marine Hospital,—thus occupying a post which the then extensive commerce of Newport rendered both lucrative and important.

He was one of the founders of the Rhode Island Medical Society, long one of its distinguished officers, and once delivered before it an oration. In 1834, in consequence of exposure, he was attacked with severe illness, and in the hope of alleviating the pains of incurable disease, he, at the earnest solicitation of his children, residing in Charleston, revisited his native city. Nearly exhausted by his disorder and by the toils of his journey, he reached it in December, 1824. For nearly a month, he lingered, with unclouded mind, and after having taken an affectionate leave of his children, and uttered his dying requests, he expired on the 21st of January, 1835, aged fifty-five years and twenty-seven days. In accordance with both his promise to his wife before her death, and his own expressed desire, his remains were, in the following April, removed to Newport, and attended by two of his sons, were deposited in the same tomb with hers, beneath the shadow of Trinity Church, in which they had for years been fellow-worshippers.

In deference to the wish of his surviving relatives, his many friends in Newport refrained from expressing their respect for the memory of their old and beloved physician, by a public funeral. The common sentiment had, however, already found fit utterance, in an obituary notice from the pen of a brother physician, published in the Newport Mercury, February, 1835. "He commenced his professional career," (says the writer,) "in this town, at an early age, and by the aid of superior talents, diligent attention, acuteness of observation, and uncommonly correct judgment, soon acquired an extensive practice, and maintained to the close of his labors, the very first rank among his brethren. As a gentleman,—the high-minded, honorable gentleman,—Dr. Waring took a stand that brooked no compromise with meanness or dishonesty, and consulted professional interest or popularity, by no appeals to vulgar prejudice or ignorant credulity. His mind was of a superior order, and he had a self-command, a kind of philosophizing and reasoning with himself, that enabled him to meet the trials and emergencies of life, with a calm dignity and composure, which we had almost said none but himself possessed, and which abode with and sustained him at the close of life. Numerous friends in this community deeply sympathize with his bereaved family." To these traits of personal and professional character, thus justly portrayed, Dr. Waring added that peculiar courtesy and suavity of manner which is so important in his profession, and which, itself, often "doeth good like a medicine." With a high sense of honor, and a dignity which commanded the respect of his brethren, a skill as a physician which won the confidence of his patients, and a gentlemanly character which attracted the regard of all his fellow citizens, he lived in the home of his adoption universally beloved, and died universally lamented. D.

Dr. DAVID KING was born in Raynham, Mass., in the year 1774. His ancestry were of Puritan origin, and were distinguished for their public spirit, and for their Christian and social virtues. His early life was passed amid influences auspicious to the growth of the best elements of character. He was prepared for college, at a grammar school, under the direction of the Rev. Peres Fobes, LL. D., a man remarkable for his peculiar eloquence and for his various learning, who officiated as President of Rhode Island College, in 1786, and was subsequently Professor of Natural Philosophy. In September, 1792, Dr. King entered Rhode Island College, as a student, under the Presidency of Manning, and graduated in 1796, under the Presidency of Maxcy. During his collegiate course, he ever received the approbation of the presiding officers of the institution, and, indeed, won the friendship of these distinguished men, for whom he was accustomed, through life, to express the highest respect and admiration. He won, too, the sincere respect of his classmates, many of whom rose, subsequently, to distinction, as Hon. Tristam Burges, of Rhode Island, Hon. John Holmes, of Maine, Hon. Asa Aldis, Chief Justice of Vermont, Abraham Blanding, a distinguished lawyer of South Carolina, Dr. Benjamin Shurtleff, of Boston, and Dr. Benjamin B. Simmons, of Charleston, South Carolina. After graduating, choosing medicine for his profession, he, together with his classmate, Shurtleff, became the pupil of Dr. James Thatcher, of Plymouth, Mass. Dr. Thatcher had officiated as Surgeon, in the revolutionary army, and his skill and experience, at this period, commanded an extensive practice in Plymouth county.

Dr. King, by his diligence and assiduity in his medical studies, soon acquired the necessary elements of a medical education. Diverted by some accidental circumstance from the navy, to which he was inclined to enter as Surgeon, he, in the autumn of 1799, sought professional employment in Newport, Rhode Island. At this time, there were but two medical practitioners in Newport, Dr. Benjamin Mason and Dr.

Jonathan Easton. Dr. Isaac Senter had just died, after a comparatively short but brilliant medical career, marked throughout by unmistakable evidences of the bold, judicious surgeon, and the wise and discriminating physician.

To attain public confidence, in a field of practice illustrated by the labors of such a man as Senter, required in the practitioner substantial merit. Dr. King fully comprehended the extent and variety of medical knowledge, demanded for this purpose. Having acquired the habits of a student during his collegiate course, he vigorously concentrated his powers upon a single object,—the attainment of a thorough knowledge of his profession. In this he was aided by the valuable library of the late Dr. Senter, which came into his possession soon after his settlement in Newport.* His mind was eminently practical, and endowed with those potent powers of execution, which are necessary to arrive at truth in any science or art. His professional knowledge was, therefore, such as to give him a just claim to the attention of his fellow citizens; this added to the kindliness of his heart, his gentlemanly deportment, his pleasing and unassuming manners, opened to him, almost from the first, an extensive practice. His practice was marked by the exercise of a sound, discriminating judgment, precision in pathological and therapeutical views, an earnest professional interest in the case, and a warm, true hearted sympathy with the patient. In cases of difficulty, his resolution and judgment ever showed a manly confidence in the resources of his own mind. The University at which he was educated evinced their high estimation of his professional character, by conferring on him, in 1821, the honorary degree of M. D.

In the early period of his professional career, his attention

---

* It contained the manuscript lectures of Cline, Haygarth and Astley Cooper; the admirable physiological treatises of Haller and Whytt; Morgagni on Pathology; fine copies of John and William Hunter's works, and the complete works of Cullen, whose rational theory and practical views may justly be said to have created a new era in medical science.

was drawn to the consideration of the vaccine disease, then first introduced into the United States. Regarding it as an invaluable discovery, he proceeded, notwithstanding the strong opposition of popular prejudice, to benefit his fellow citizens by the application of the newly discovered principle in his science.*

In thus early adopting the views of the immortal Jenner, and carrying them out in practice, he displayed a decision and independence of mind, which strongly characterized him through life.

For several years he held the appointment of Surgeon to a detachment of United States troops stationed at Fort Wolcott. In 1819, during the prevalence of the yellow fever in this place, his great skill and experience was actively and successfully called into operation, in repelling that terrible malady. At that time, it was the part of humanity to refute the errors of those who regarded that disease as invariably and certainly propagating itself, and as exposing those who attended upon the sick, to almost certain death. Not admitting the contagious character of the disease, he attributed it to a more general and pervading cause; and by his intrepidity, and free personal exposure, attested his confidence in the truth of his theoretical views.

In 1827, that enlightened champion of non-contagion, M. Cherrin, visited Newport, held several conferences with Dr. King, with regard to his experience of the epidemic of 1819, and obtained his decided testimony in favor of the non-contagiousness of yellow fever.†

Ardently attached to his profession, he was ever ready to promote all useful and liberal plans, which might contribute to the improvement and elevation of its character. He was

---

* In October, 1800, Dr. King vaccinated Walter Cornell, of Newport, who was the first person vaccinated in the State of Rhode Island.

† M. Cherrin obtained a similar testimony from Drs. Waring, Turner and Case. Dr. E. Hazard gave his evidence in favor of the doctrine of contagion.

one of the earliest promoters of the Rhode Island Medical Society, in which he successively held the offices of Censor, Vice President and President. He was elected President in June, 1830, and continued in that office until July, 1834.

During his presidency, he delivered an inaugural discourse, illustrating the true means of advancing medical science.

But his profession did not usurp all his attention. He was always a friend and advocate of those means of public improvement, by which the feelings of a community are liberalized, and an impulse is given to its moral, as well as physical energies. The same practical understanding and active energy, which he devoted to his profession, were exhibited in the promotion of the various institutions with which he was connected, so that wherever he acted, his influence was felt. In the revival of Redwood Library, in 1840, he was an active coöperator, with other public spirited men, and he was long a director, and at last President of that institution, until ill health compelled him to resign that office.

It was his pride to advance those enterprises which might benefit the town in which he lived; and he regarded it with an attachment which, in general, is appropriated only to the spot of our birth. It will be observed, that he sometimes turned aside from those avocations which were strictly professional, to duties and services of a general nature. But it is not to be regretted, that he should have sunk the more exclusive and narrow aim of mere professional ambition, in the more universal character of a citizen. It was the necessary result of his character, in which moral impulses predominated. It sprung from that principle which made him the friend, as well as the physician of his patients, and to their pecuniary obligations superadded a debt of gratitude. It was the result, too, of public confidence, which reposed its trusts in his hands, and felt that they were as secure as integrity could make them.

His mind was distinguished for that due proportion between the various faculties, which leads to their harmonious action, and which subdued in him, all these exaggerations of character and feeling, which are so eccentric and imposing. To such regularity did this constitution of mind lead, in the ordinary intercourse of life, as to make the uniform discharge of duty seem more a happiness of his nature, than a self-constrained virtue. An union of simplicity and firmness, a love of the liberal, the true and the useful, and a conscientious adherence to what he judged to be right, made him a model for the citizen.

The uprightness of his character, and the strength of his judgment, induced many to consult him as a friend, to whom, notwithstanding the pressing cares of his professional life, he rendered valuable services. The warm sensibilities of his heart ever prompted him to disinterested action, which made him the object of preëminent respect while living, and will forever perpetuate his memory in the hearts of his friends. In private life, his character was adorned by every quality which constitutes goodness.

A perfect faith in God was ever an ennobling presence in his mind. The practice of his art was to him a privilege, as involving the exercise of his higher nature. He understood the great truth expressed by the moral poet of the age: —

> "How, on earth,
> Man, if he do but live within the light
> Of high endeavors, daily spreads abroad
> His being, armed with the strength that cannot fail."

His daily prayer to the Spirit on high was —

> "Instruct me, for Thou knowest;
> What in me is dark, illume;
> What is low, raise and support."

Such was the religious character of this true and single-hearted man.

In August, 1834, he suffered an attack of paralysis, brought on from exertions in the discharge of his professional duties. His constitution gradually failed until his death, which occurred November 14th, 1836. When he had thus been struck down, in the midst of active life, the attachment of the community to him was most signally exhibited. Throughout the community there was an universal conviction, that society had lost a benefactor,—an invaluable member. In the extensive circle of his own patients, there pervaded a feeling of personal loss which no other person could supply. Few men have lived more respected, or died more lamented.

[DAVID KING, M. D.]

Dr. BENJAMIN W. CASE was a popular physician in Newport; but want of material facts compels us to defer noticing him for the present.

In a performance like the present, depending for its materials on traditionary information, it would be strange if there are not many errors, both of omission and commission. However numerous these may be, it is due to the other members of the committee, Drs. Ray and Collins, to exonerate them from blame or responsibility, they having left its entire execution in the hands of the chairman.

---

## MEDICAL EDUCATION IN RHODE ISLAND.

The general practice in the education of physicians, prior to the organization of the Medical Society, in 1812, was, for pupils to enter their names as apprentices, in some physician's office. Among the teachers most patronized in this way, were those already mentioned, in Newport; and Drs. William and Pardon Bowen and Levi Wheaton, in Providence; Drs. Babcock, of Westerly, Whitridge, of Tiverton, and Fiske and Anthony, of Scituate. The teachers gave the pupil a letter of recommendation, on leaving, which was his only credential. After the Society was organized, a few pupils were examined and licensed by its censors. No pupils, except the Bowens, attended medical lectures. In 1800, there were not five medical graduates in the State. At the present day, there are not five physicians of respectable standing, in the State, who have not graduated as doctors of medicine.

The first schools opened in the country, were in Philadelphia, in 1762; in New York, 1768; in Boston, 1780, and in Hanover, in 1800. In 1810, one was opened in Providence in connection with Brown University; Drs. William Ingalls, Levi Wheaton, Solomon Drowne and William C. Bowen being appointed professors. The first named gentleman and the last, gave two courses of lectures on anatomy and surgery, and chemistry, which were all that the college then required of candidates for medical degrees. Dr. Ingalls then transferred his lectures to Boston, where they were continued till 1822, when the school was reörganized at the college, in Providence, under the following professors: —

Levi Wheaton, M. D., on Theory and Practice of Physic, and Obstetrics.

John DeWolf, on Chemistry.

Solomon Drowne, M. D., on Materia Medica and Botany.

Usher Parsons, M. D., Anatomy, Physiology and Surgery.

From 1822 to 1826, the number of pupils ranged between twenty and fifty, most of whom received the degree of Doctor of Medicine. It was, however, found that the proximity of medical schools in Boston, New Haven and Pittsfield, which were provided with ample accommodations, would always prevent the growth and success of one in Rhode Island, and the school was therefore abandoned in 1826. The Professor of Anatomy, who had given a short course of lectures annually, to the upper classes in the college, since 1822, continued them till 1828, when these also ceased.

Medical literature has received very few contributions in Rhode Island. The medical journals of Philadelphia, New York and Boston have received some communications, and in early times, some were sent to European journals. One of these, by Dr. Senter, of Newport, is often quoted by foreign writers.

---

## FISKE FUND PRIZE ESSAYS.

The Fiske fund has produced many prize essays, about half of them written in Rhode Island; they were as follows:—

1835. 1. What are the causes and nature of Rheumatism, and the best mode of treatment to be employed therein?

Award of forty dollars to THOMAS H. WEBB.

2. What are the causes and nature of Purpura Hemorrhagica, and the best mode of treatment to be employed therein?

Award of forty dollars to DAVID KING, M. D., of Newport.

1836. 3. What are the causes and nature of Cholera Infantum, and the best mode of treatment to be employed therein?

Award of forty dollars to DAVID KING, M. D., of Newport.

4. What are the nature and best mode of treatment of Delirium Tremens?

Award of forty dollars to JACOB FULLER, M. D., of Providence.

1837. 5. What are the causes, nature and best mode of treatment of Scarlatina Anginosa?

Award of forty dollars to JACOB FULLER, M. D.

1838. 6. What are the varieties and best mode of treatment of Syphilis?

Award of fifty dollars to DAVID KING, M. D., Newport.

1841. 7. What are the causes, character and nature of the diseases of the spine, both structural and functional, and what is the best mode of treatment to be employed in each?

Award of one hundred dollars to USHER PARSONS, M. D.

1842. 8. What are the causes, character, nature and best mode of treatment of Asthma?

Award of fifty dollars to JOSHUA B. CHAPIN, M. D., Providence.

1844. 9. Tenotomy; its comparative advantages and disadvantages?

Award of fifty dollars to JOSHUA B. CHAPIN, M. D.

1844. 10. The best mode of treating, and the best apparatus for the management of fractures of the thigh.

Award of fifty dollars to WILLIAM E. COALE, M. D., Boston.

1847. 11. Vis Medicatrix Naturæ; how far should it be relied on in the treatment of diseases?

Award of fifty dollars to C. W. PARSONS, M. D.

1848. 12. Ship fever; its nature and best modes of treatment.

Award of fifty dollars to HENRY GRAFTON CLARK, M. D., of Boston.

1849. 13. The history of Medical Delusions of the present and former times.

Award of fifty dollars to WORTHINGTON HOOKER, M. D., of Norwich, Conn.

1850. 14. Homeopathy, so called; its history and refutation.

Award of fifty dollars to WORTHINGTON HOOKER, M. D., Norwich, Conn.

1851. 15. Displacement of the Uterus; its local and constitutional effects, and best mode of treatment.

Award of fifty dollars to J. F. PEEBLES, M. D., Petersburg, Va.

1853. 16. Neuralgia; its history and best mode of treatment.

Award of fifty dollars to C. W. PARSONS, M. D., Providence.

1854. 17. Croup.

Award of fifty dollars to ALBERT NEWMAN, M. D., Attleboro, Mass.

1854. 18. Effects of climate on tubercular disease.

Award of one hundred dollars, to EDWIN LEE, M. D., of London.

1855. 19. Does pregnancy accelerate or retard tubercular disease in the lungs, in persons predisposed to this disease?

Award of one hundred dollars, to EDWIN WARREN, M. D., Edenton, N. C.

1856. 20. What are the causes and nature of that disease, incident to pregnancy and lactation, characterized by inflammation and ulceration of the mouth and fauces, by anorexia and emaciation and diarrhœa, and what is the best mode of treatment?

Award of one hundred dollars to DAVID HUTCHINSON, M. D., Mooresville, Indiana.

1858. 21. The effects of the use of alcoholic liquors on tubercular disease, or in constitutions predisposed to such disease; supported by facts, presented, as far as possible, in statistical form.

Award of two hundred dollars to JOHN BELL, M. D., of New York, June 1st, 1859.

| | |
|---|---|
| The whole number of questions proposed, has been | 42 |
| Premiums awarded, - - - - | 21 |
| Premiums within the State, - - - | 11 |
| Premiums out of the State, - - - | 10 |

The Fiske fund supplies each fellow with a copy of every

essay, and many copies for distribution abroad. It is believed that the fund for awarding premiums, generously bequeathed by Dr. Caleb Fiske, will call into exercise the literary and medical abilities of the junior physicians, and advance the cause of medical science throughout the State.

There is no public hospital in the State. An Almshouse or Asylum for the poor, was built twenty-five years ago, by the munificence of Knight Dexter, Esquire, which affords to the attending physicians some field for hospital practice.

The Butler Hospital for the Insane is a noble institution, erected by the munificence of the late Cyrus Butler and Nicholas Brown, and many others. It has been, since first opened, under the superintendence of Isaac Ray, M. D.

Revision of the National Pharmacopœia.—Every ten years, a meeting of delegates from the several State Medical Societies has been held, generally at Philadelphia, for the purpose of revising the Pharmacopœia of the United States. This Society has usually chosen delegates.

American Medical Association.—This Society has taken an active part in its meetings, which are held annually, in different cities, by sending delegates; and it has substituted the system of Medical Ethics of that body for its own By-Laws, so far as they are applicable.

---

## REGISTRATION REPORTS.

The Society has taken a prominent part in procuring the establishment of a systematic registration of births, marriages and deaths, in this State. Several laws had formerly existed on this subject; but they were almost wholly ineffectual,—entirely so in regard to the collection of statistics from the State at large. At the annual meeting of this Society, in June, 1850, Dr. Mauran brought this subject to its attention;

and, on his motion, a special committee was appointed to act in connection with the appropriate committee of the General Assembly. The subsequent enactment of the earliest effective law on this subject, was obtained at the suggestion, and under the advice, of this committee of the Medical Society; and at all stages of its progress, the efforts of the chairman, Dr. Mauran, were most assiduous, and finally successful. The statistics of births, marriages and deaths, are now very carefully collected,—more thoroughly, we believe, than in any other State, except Massachusetts, which took the lead in this important public movement. The returns for each year are, according to the law, made the subject of annual reports, the preparation of which is confided to a committee of our Society, chosen for the purpose. Five annual reports have already been published, and widely circulated among medical men throughout the country; and the Medical Society has the satisfaction of seeing this system permanently established in Rhode Island, through the efforts of its own members, and the control of many of its details placed in their hands. The first report was prepared by Thomas H. Webb, M. D., and the four subsequent ones, by Charles W. Parsons, M. D., of Providence.

A pamphlet, containing the act of incorporation, list of petitioners for the same, in 1812, by-laws, medical police, account of the Fiske fund, and a catalogue of the officers and fellows, is published every three years.

The charter authorizes the members of the Society to elect the necessary officers, and to determine their duties; to hold a common seal, with power to break or change it; to sue and be sued; to enact rules and by-laws, and annex fines and penalties; to determine the number necessary to constitute a quorum, and to establish the time, place and manner of convening the Society; to elect, by a majority of the votes of those present, suitable persons as members and honorary members,—the former to subscribe to the by-laws within one year, or otherwise declare their assent in writing,—the latter to consist of persons residing out of the State, or not practicing in it; to examine candidates for the practice of physic and surgery, and if found qualified, to give them letters testimonial; and to hold real estate, yielding an annual income of not exceeding five hundred dollars, and of personal estate not exceeding fifteen hundred dollars.

The by-laws specify:— 1. That annual meetings shall be held at Providence, on the first Wednesday in June, at 10 o'clock A. M., at such place as the President may appoint, fourteen days' notice being previously given in some paper printed in the city of Providence, and also by a written or printed notice, addressed to each Fellow of the Society, by the Recording Secretary; at which meeting ten Fellows shall constitute a quorum for the transaction of business.

There shall also be a semi-annual meeting, held on the third Wednesday in December, at 10 o'clock A. M., at such town or city as the Society, at its previous annual meeting, may appoint, notice to be given as for the annual meeting.

The whole number of Fellows admitted, prior to 1850, is 212.

Officers of the Society from its commencement, in 1812, to 1850:—

PRESIDENTS.

| | | | |
|---|---|---|---|
| Amos Throop, | 1812 to 1814. | Lewis L. Miller, | 1846 to 1847. |
| William Bowen, | 1814 to 1815. | Joseph Mauran, | 1847 to 1848. |
| Pardon Bowen. | 1815 to 1823. | David King, | 1848 to 1849. |
| Caleb Fiske, | 1823 to 1824. | S. Aug. Arnold, | 1849 to 1850. |
| Levi Wheaton, | 1824 to 1829. | George Capron, | 1850 to 1851. |
| David King, | 1829 to 1834. | Hiram Allen, | 1851 to 1852. |
| Charles Eldredge, | 1834 to 1837. | Joseph Mauran, | 1852 to 1855. |
| Usher Parsons, | 1837 to 1840. | Ariel Ballou, | 1855 to 1856. |
| Richmond Brownell, | 1840 to 1843. | Isaac Ray, | 1856 to 1858. |
| Theophilus C. Dunn. | 1843 to 1846. | Jas. H. Eldredge, | 1858 to 1860. |

## FIRST VICE PRESIDENTS.

| | | | |
|---|---|---|---|
| Wm. Bowen, | 1812 to 1813. | Jabez Holmes, | 1846 to 1847. |
| Peter Turner, | 1813 to 1815. | David King, | 1847 to 1848. |
| William Whitridge, | 1815 to 1818. | S. Aug. Arnold, | 1848 to 1849. |
| Caleb Fiske, | 1818 to 1823. | Geo. Capron, | 1849 to 1850. |
| David King, | 1823 to 1829. | Hiram Allen, | 1850 to 1851. |
| Solomon Drowne, | 1829 to 1830. | William A. Shaw, | 1851 to 1852. |
| John Mackie, | 1831 to 1833. | Sylvanus Clapp, | 1852 to 1854. |
| Samuel West, | 1833 to 1837. | Ariel Ballou, | 1854 to 1855. |
| William Turner, | 1837 to 1838. | Hiram Cleaveland, | 1855 to 1856. |
| Niles Manchester, | 1838 to 1840. | James H. Eldredge, | 1856 to 1858. |
| Theophilus C. Dunn, | 1840 to 1843. | Charles W. Parsons, | 1858 to 1860. |
| Lewis L. Miller. | 1843 to 1846. | | |

## SECOND VICE PRESIDENTS.

| | | | |
|---|---|---|---|
| Jonathan Easton, | 1812 to 1813. | David King, | 1846 to 1847. |
| Peter Turner, | 1813 to 1814. | S. Aug. Arnold, | 1847 to 1848. |
| Pardon Bowen, | 1814 to 1815. | George Capron, | 1848 to 1849. |
| Caleb Fiske, | 1815 to 1819. | Hiram Allen, | 1849 to 1850. |
| David King, | 1819 to 1823. | Wm. A. Shaw, | 1850 to 1851. |
| Solomon Drowne, | 1824 to 1829. | Joseph Mauran, | 1851 to 1852. |
| John Mackie, | 1829 to 1831. | Chas. W. Parsons, | 1852 to 1853. |
| Edmund T. Waring, | 1831 to 1834. | Ariel Ballou, | 1853 to 1854. |
| William G. Shaw, | 1834 to 1837. | Hiram Cleaveland, | 1854 to 1855. |
| Ezekiel Fowler, | 1837 to 1840. | Isaac Ray. | 1855 to 1856. |
| Jere. Williams, | 1840 to 1842. | Chas. W. Parsons, | 1856 to 1858. |
| Lewis L. Miller, | 1842 to 1843. | Henry E. Turner, | 1858 to 1860. |
| Jabez Holmes, | 1843 to 1846. | | |

## RECORDING SECRETARIES.

| | | | |
|---|---|---|---|
| John Mackie, | 1812 to 1817. | C. G. Perry, | 1844 to 1846. |
| J. W. Richmond, | 1817 to 1821. | C. W. Parsons, | 1846 to 1849. |
| Pardon Brownell, | 1821 to 1825. | J. W. C. Ely, | 1849 to 1852. |
| Richmond Brownell, | 1825 to 1830. | Edwin M. Snow, | 1852 to 1855. |
| S. Aug. Arnold, | 1830 to 1837. | W. O. Brown, | 1855 to 1858. |
| Johnson Gardner, | 1837 to 1842. | J. H. Rathbone, | 1858 to 1859. |
| Leander Utley, | 1842 to 1844. | Edward A. Crane, | 1859 to 1860. |

## CORRESPONDING SECRETARIES.

| | | | |
|---|---|---|---|
| William Turner, | 1812 to 1832. | Henry E. Turner, | 1851 to 1852. |
| Thomas H. Webb, | 1832 to 1839. | J. W. C. Ely, | 1852 to 1855. |
| C. G. Perry, | 1839 to 1840. | Edwin M. Snow, | 1855 to 1856. |
| Hiram Allen, | 1840 to 1849. | George P. Baker, | 1856 to 1860. |
| C. W. Parsons, | 1849 to 1851. | | |

## TREASURERS.

| | | | |
|---|---|---|---|
| Thos. M. Barrows, | 1812 to 1830. | Lewis W. Clifford, | 1849 to 1850. |
| Jacob Fuller, | 1830 to 1839. | Chas. W. Fabyan, | 1850 to 1852. |
| Sylvester Knight, | 1839 to 1841. | George P. Baker, | 1852 to 1855. |
| H. Armington, | 1841 to 1849. | George L. Collins, | 1855 to 1860. |